THE MOLE BROTHERS' MAGNIFICENT MISSION

MINERVA TAYLOR

ISBN: 1453831568
ISBN-13: 9781453831564

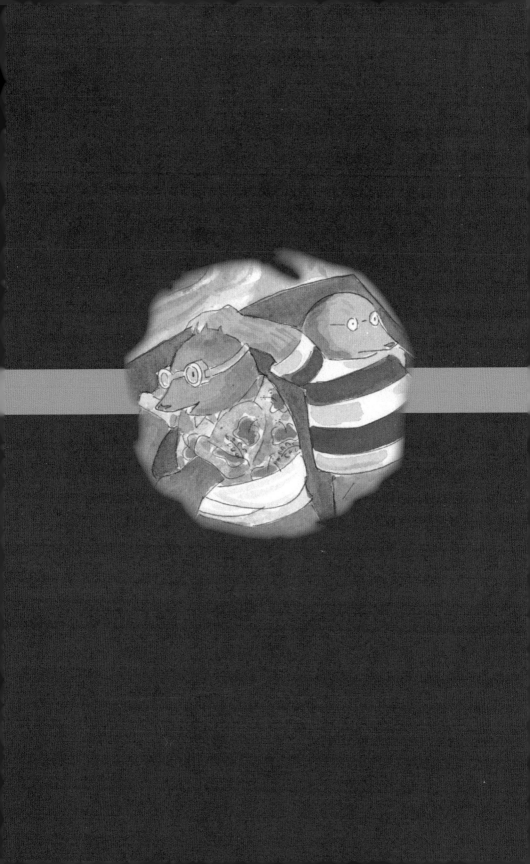

CHAPTER ONE

Once upon a time there was a colony of moles that lived two feet underneath a seaside village about eighty miles from New York City. The moles had fled the city two hundred mole years ago when their tunnels were invaded by vicious street rats. Since then, life near the ocean had been happy and peaceful for them.

James Mole thought about all this underground history as he waited for his older brother Stewart to take him to the library. Our mole way of life may be coming to an end, he said to himself. His long sharp nose quivered with emotion, and a few tears crept out of his tiny nearsighted eyes.

Stewart rushed up beside him.

"Sorry I'm late." His black fur stood up in little points on his head as it always did when he was in a hurry. "I found some delicious grubs on the way and stopped for a snack." He patted his little brother with his short front paw. The kid's scared, he thought, and so am I.

Last night the brothers had sneaked out to the emergency meeting held in the town hall. Creeping up against the door, they placed their paws and tails down on the floor to listen.

Mayor Burrows' low gravelly voice vibrated through the floor. "Mole Town is in great danger. We are being overrun by summer people above us. The humans are buying up more land and building more houses with swimming pools, smooth lawns and tennis courts. They are destroying our mole community, knocking out entire areas of our town." There were frightened murmurs and shouts from the crowd. Melissa Mole shrieked in terror and had to be carried out of the hall for air.

The Mayor's voice shook with anger. "Why only last week the northeast corner of the Mole Elementary School grounds was crushed by another bulldozer digging yet another pool. These abovegrounders also have a strange wish for the perfect lawn and garden. Our beautiful shafts just are not acceptable to them. Lucy and Bud Darkly were blasted right out of their kitchen by some fanatic up there wanting everything smooth. Now Police Chief Black would like to have a word about security."

The brothers almost could see the Chief twirl his whiskers with his very wide front paws, the widest in the entire mole town, as he spoke, "I am sad to report that no place, not even under the Field Club grounds, is safe anymore. Warn your children not to touch any of the poison being placed near our tunnels. Other emergency actions have been taken. We are burrowing in safer areas by the edge of the road and near houses which are not being used. But we are running out of space and can't rely on these measures. We must find a way to stop the senseless building above us or we will perish."

Squeaks of alarm filled the hall.

Mayor Burrows ended the meeting on a fur-raising note. "We must think of something. Our next meeting will be held in three days if we're still here."

Even after the meeting, the brothers couldn't really believe they were in serious danger until they peeked into the kitchen that night and overhead their parents. Mama's short curls wiggled as she cried softly.

"What shall we do? We love this place and know all the smells from the sea and the bay. The children will be so unhappy if we are forced to move. We might have to scatter to different strange places. It could even mean our lives will be in danger."

Then Mama stamped her paw. "It's those wretched summer people! Why, the whole place rattles down here from their cars and cuisinarts."

"Don't get excited now." Papa, a very large black mole, a little plump around the middle, tried to comfort her. The brothers knew he was very upset. His jogging path had been cut up so the humans could plant a hedge. "We'll think of something."

"Think of something," James begged his older brother as they scurried along the tunnel toward the library. Stewart always had the answers to any problem.

"Yeah, but it isn't easy. Stay away from that white glob; it might be poison!" he shouted.

James broke into a howl.

Stewart slammed him on the fat part of his back with his short paw. "Quiet, the humans up there might hear you squeaking."

At the library story hour, James had trouble listening, even though Miss Hollow, the librarian, was reading about a human boy who loved animals. He watched Stewart digging around in the reference shelf of the library. James was not comforted by the fact that he knew something the other little moles didn't.

He didn't even shriek with laughter as he usually did when his friend Sam began

pulling books off the shelf, and Hillary began throwing cards out of the catalogue, making Miss Hollow very angry.

Stewart was peering closely at a large piece of paper. James strained to see, opening his eyes as wide as he could until Miss Hollow in a cross voice asked, "James, why aren't you paying attention?" He sank back, biting his tiny pointed lips while his friends giggled.

Then, just as Miss Hollow got to the good part where the boy had been caught in an animal trap, they heard a rumble overhead. Miss Hollow snapped the book shut and said briskly, "Home now. Library's closed. It's dangerous." She hurried the squealing little moles out toward the main tunnel. The walls about the room began to crumble.

Miss Hollow screamed, "Another tennis court!" as she scurried through the tunnel that led to the Police Station.

After seeing that the smaller moles scrambled home safely, the brothers continued on, puffing with excitement.

James noticed that Stewart had something tucked under his right paw.

"What's that?"

"Tell you later," was all he would say.

At home Mama and Papa were in the bedroom getting ready to go out. The boys couldn't believe it, at a time like this. Papa was changing from his striped vest to his navy jacket which made him look slimmer.

"Mama, Papa," they shouted, "the library just caved in."

Papa's sloping brow creased in anger. "This is urgent. We must have the town meeting tomorrow," he said.

"Oh dear, something must be done. Soon there will be no place for us. We surely are in danger." Mama was in front of the mirror, putting on eye shadow to make her tiny slits

of eyes look bigger. "Perhaps we shouldn't go. But it is Mimsey's birthday, and Roger has planned this party for months. We're just not going to be terrorized and stay home." Her mouth was a firm white line underneath her lipstick. She turned to the brothers. "Boys, your dinner is on the table. And James, I expect you to be in bed at seven-thirty."

James pushed out his lower lip. He was furious. Their whole world was crumbling and Mama still expected him to go to bed early.

In the kitchen, Stewart just managed to take the mysterious roll of paper from under his paw and hide it in the breadbox before his parents bustled in to say goodbye.

"Hurry dear, we're late," Papa said, giving James a stern look. James stamped his back paws. He always squeaked a lot about going to bed.

Stewart knew by his brother's wrinkled up nose that he was working himself into a tantrum which would delay his parents and his secret mission. Stewart nudged him and winked. And knowing something was up, James kept quiet.

A soon as their parents left for the main tunnel, Stewart turned to his brother. "I've got an idea. What a break they've gone out. It gives us time."

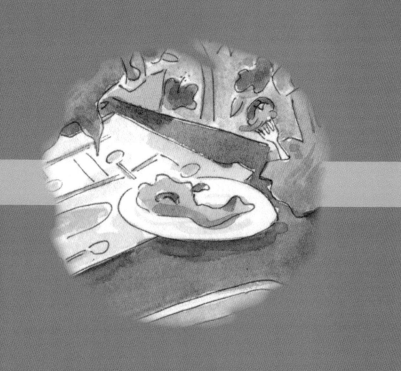

CHAPTER TWO
THE MISSION

The brothers sat down to the earthworm casserole and root salad Mama had prepared for them. James dawdled over the last bites.

"Hurry, eat it all. You need all the strength you can get." Stewart reached in the breadbox and brought out the rolled-up piece of paper he had carried out of the library. "I didn't check this out with Miss Hollow, but in the emergency I didn't think she'd mind."

"What is it?" James asked, still dangling a few worms on his fork.

Stewart unrolled it and smoothed it out on the table. "It's an official Mole Ordinance Map. It shows all the human property divisions, our burrows and natural markings in this area."

"Wow! Where's our burrow?"

"Here." Stewart pointed to a spot on the map under Main Street.

"But what does this have to do with our problem?"

Stewart munched the last few worms on James' plate before he answered, "We've always had to adapt to the humans above us because many of them don't notice or care about the animals who live around them. We must find a place near to our lovely town that no human up there wants and rebuild our tunnels."

"Hey, you ate my dinner. That's not fair," James yelled and gave his brother a whack on the nose. But too curious to fight, he went on. "There aren't any places, except very far away from our town. We'll all be scattered or..." He gulped and tried not to think about what else might happen.

"I've found a place." Stewart pointed to some vacant lots in a field above the ground south of Main Street.

"But bulldozers are digging there," James said.

"I know, I know, but if you look closely, you'll see an underground spring."

James' brow wrinkled as he put his nose on the table to get a good look.

"Notice," said Stewart. His index claw tapped at the map. "The stream is on higher ground than that field with those empty lots. It is kept on course by a wall of rock and earth."

"Oh yes, I see, but isn't that high? It looks like a hill, an enormous one."

"Yes, it is high. We have to tunnel down to the stream and find places in the wall of earth to burrow so that it collapses. Then the spring will be released and flood the field so the humans will be forced to stop building there." He pointed with his claw. "Just beyond that field is a small piece of higher ground, not large enough for homes or swimming pools. We can tunnel around the flood water and move Mole Town under there. Then we will be safe from the humans."

James let out a whistle between the gaps in his front teeth. "That's clever, but that field is all torn up by the bulldozers, a No Mole Land. We'll have to go above ground." His small plump body shivered with fear.

All sorts of terrors lurked above ground. Once he had been too near the surface and was uncovered by a hoe with a human at the other end. He had managed to burrow underground quickly to escape. And Stewart just missed being run down by a bicycle when he accidentally popped up near the road.

"I'd rather stay home," James said in a trembling voice. His claws shook as he put his glass down on the table.

"All right, I'll do it myself. I'll save the town. It would be easier to have someone dig with me. As it is, it will take all night."

"But I'm not allowed more than one foot toward the above ground, and I'm supposed to be in bed at seven-thirty," James whimpered.

For a moment Stewart lost heart. His brother was right to be afraid. Every day or two Papa would warn, "Never, ever go above ground. You surely will be killed by the humans who think of us as useless creatures. Remember what happened to Cousin Eddie."

Cousin Eddie was their cousin on their mother's side. Eddie had been a curious, reckless mole. A few years ago he made one too many trips above ground and never returned. For weeks after his disappearance Mayor Burrows sent out night search parties. The only trace of Eddie they found was his pair of broken eye glasses lying beside the road.

Realizing what was at risk, Stewart's courage returned. Placing his front paws on each side of James' neck, he looked at him solemnly. "This is our mission. We must try to save our town. You know how grown-ups behave. They'll form all kinds of committees, argue a lot and in the meantime, our tunnels and burrows will disappear. We can't wait for them to come up with an answer." His pointy jaw jutted out, looking almost square.

"Okay, I'll go," James said reluctantly. All he really wanted to do was cuddle in his rootlet bed.

"Then, let's get a move on."

CHAPTER THREE
ABOVE GROUND

The brothers scurried through the main tunnel for as long as they could until they reached the empty lots where the ground was all topsy-turvy. They burrowed upward, and then a swift warm breeze hit them. They were above ground! Smells were different, full of danger. They caught the scent of the ocean and heard its roar. Something howled in the distance. And the space was so vast, beautiful in a way. Bright lights sparkled in the dark sky. But which way to go now? Shadows loomed. They wiggled their noses in the air.

"Come on," Stewart whispered.

James followed along past the giant machines that were used to build human houses. He shivered. It wasn't cozy and safe out here. There was a wildness that frightened him. As they passed another bulldozer, James realized that the howling had stopped. He pulled at his brother's pink tail.

"Stop that." Stewart was angry and frightened. The ground was very rough, and he wasn't sure he was going in the right direction.

James' paws vibrated. He heard snuffling sounds close behind him which made the smooth hairs on his back stand up straight.

"Stewart, Stewart," he hissed.

As they turned, an enormous black dog with teeth like daggers lunged at them. They scurried behind the track of the bulldozer. There was no time to dig to safety. The dog jumped at them, snapping and snarling. They huddled together. Their entire mole

lives flashed before them. Soon the vicious animal would be around the wheel.

"Follow me," Stewart squeaked, "Don't look back, just follow me." He pushed himself up over the track of the bulldozer onto a narrow bar that led to its huge scoop. The black beast, so close that James could see into his open jaws, leapt at them, his teeth grazing their tails. They heard him floundering after them in the darkness, barking furiously.

Slowly, slowly they crept along toward the bulldozer's large scoop. "Don't look back," Stewart kept repeating, for if they fell, those terrible jaws would be waiting.

Too terrified to squeal, James struggled to keep on the slippery bar. He was used to digging, not climbing. His tiny claws clicked on the cold steel as he slipped backward, then scrambled forward with all his strength, keeping up with his big brother's hunched back.

When they reached a wider section of the machine, Stewart took a deep breath and bravely jumped into the large scoop, then reached out and pulled James in. They were safe. Both of them lay flat, dizzy from their escape. The dog had stopped barking, but he still lurked down there.

They waited in the large scoop, listening, sniffing and gazing into the endless darkness. Once more their enemy hurled himself at them and fell back on the ground, then paced back and forth below, growling under his breath. After a long time, ages in a mole's life, the dog gave up and loped away.

"Quick, he's gone." Stewart pulled his brother up. Taking deep breaths, they tumbled out of the scoop, falling into a heap upon the ground, the wind knocked from them.

Stewart scrambled up first, not giving his brother time to complain. He paused and sniffed. Not only did they have to get across this field, but they also must tunnel in the right place to find the spring.

They hurried on in the dark, stumbling over rocks and upturned trees, thinking of poor Cousin Eddie and hoping the black dog would not find them.

CHAPTER FOUR
THE ACCIDENT

"We can start digging as soon as we reach the end of this broken earth," Stewart whispered. The ground went in great dips up and down. In the dim moonlight they could see cans, papers and bottles scattered everywhere.

James didn't answer. His back paws were caught in something gooey. He had tried to free one paw from the sticky mess and now both were stuck. "Help, I can't move. What is this stuff?"

"Oh no!" Stewart clapped the side of his head with his paw. "Chewing gum. It's a curious human habit. They chew it but don't swallow it."

"I guess not," James said miserably.

Stewart took the wrapper which was still clinging to the wad and pried the gum off his brother's back paws, taking some fur with it.

"Ouch! Are you sure we'll get a reward for this?" James wished he had never agreed to come.

"Why yes, we'll save our home."

"What do you think it will be? A larva cake? Or maybe they'll let me stay up as long as I want to. It had better be good," James said.

"We'll be heroes. There might even be a parade. But come on. We won't be anything if we don't get across this field." They were worried. They had been above ground too long. Other dangerous animals like foxes and gophers would catch their scent and come after them.

Crossing the field was harder than Stewart ever imagined because of the garbage scattered everywhere. He had read that humans had a lot of leftover things they couldn't use and tossed them on the ground. Snorting through his pointed nose with anger, he dodged a greasy paper bag. "Good thing moles don't litter," he muttered to himself. "All our tunnels would be clogged."

Suddenly a sharp pain stabbed his side. "Ow!" he screeched.

"What's the matter?" James puffed, catching up with him.

Stewart flopped over on his left side between two bumps in the ground. "I'm not sure. It's my underside; it hurts a lot."

"Holey Moley! There's a piece of glass sticking out of your tummy. Must be from a broken bottle."

"Take it out James. Hurry, I can't reach it." Tears of pain slid down his cheeks. James gulped. He wasn't used to his brother depending on him, but he had to remove the glass. Using his claws on both front paws, he gingerly gripped the glass so as not to cut himself.

Stewart shrieked. The sliver of glass came out easily, but blood gushed after it. "I can't stand the sight of my own blood. I feel dizzy." His head flopped over, and he lay very still.

"He's fainted. Help me someone, anyone." James cried out. He wished with all his heart that they were safe at home. Usually when he got into trouble an adult or his brother came to the rescue. But in this deserted field there was no one to help him.

After a while he stopped crying and frantically sniffing around, found some leaves from a broken tree branch, wet with dew. He placed them on his brother's wound and held them tightly for a long time, remembering the first aid instructions he received at school. When he picked up the leaves, the wound was still bleeding, but not as much. He had to find a bandage.

Daring to go a few steps away from his brother, he searched through the trash the humans had left. Among the bottles and plastic bags, he found a piece of cloth. Human material he guessed, and shuddered. Taking it between his sharp claws, he ripped it into a long strip, long enough to go around Stewart's tummy.

Lucky that Stewart is thin, he thought. This will surely reach around. He slipped one end over the top of his brother's tummy, then lifted his back and pulled the rest around. He did this twice, grunting with exertion, and then tied the bandage with a knot.

"Water," Stewart moaned.

"Hurray, he's alive," James shouted. But then he wondered where he would find water. There was no sign of any here. He hunted in the dim light through piles of garbage, coming up with a tin can with huge colorful letters printed on it. Above grounders, he knew, drank from containers rather than streams. This must be one of their drinks. He sniffed at the opening on top of the can. It smelled harmless. He picked it up between his paws and let the sweet liquid slither down his throat. "Ugh." His face twisted in dislike. It didn't have the clear taste of water, but at least he wasn't thirsty anymore. He saved the rest for his brother.

Struggling with one paw, he brought it to Stewart, tilted his head back and poured it down his throat. He choked. "Yuk, that tastes awful." James laughed with relief.

"Have I been out long?"

"Yes." To James it seemed an eternity. "Are you ok?"

"I think so." He got to his feet slowly and examined his side. "It's stopped bleeding and doesn't hurt, thanks to you." He vowed he never again would get angry or impatient with his little brother. He gave James a pat on the back. "You were great. Now let's go."

They scurried across the field, munching some grub worms on the way to give them strength.

CHAPTER FIVE
THE GOPHERS

"When we reach the end of the field, we must dig right away. I smell a fox on our trail," Stewart whispered. They stopped to rest, wiping the sweat from their brows. In front of them was a long stretch of land which climbed upward to the hill.

"This is it," they shouted and dug quickly, their wide front paws like shovels as they piled up the dirt behind them and pushed it away with their back paws.

It was a relief to be underground again, and to their surprise, the brothers found some tunnels already made for their use.

"Gophers," Stewart muttered.

"Gophers!" James' head swiveled around to see if any were following. "Are they dangerous?"

"Too many of them together, yes, but not one at a time. They don't like trespassers. We'll have to risk it because it will save time."

They hurried through the gophers' tunnels toward the direction of the spring.

"Stop!" Stewart held out his paw.

They heard jabbering ahead and before they had time to burrow away, they came face to face with a gang of gophers.

If only it had been a mother or father gopher, but this was a gang that hung out at the video game arcade at the edge of Mole Town. They were tough mean gophers. Stewart gulped hard. The brothers were trapped.

"We're toast!" squealed James, jumping behind his brother.

The gophers leaned against each side of the tunnel walls, making it impossible for the moles to pass.

"What do ya think yer doin'?" One of the bigger gophers in a black leather jacket yelled. He was picking his large buck teeth with a sharp knife.

Stewart tried to reason with them. "We just want to pass. We won't do any harm to your tunnel."

"Hah, do you think we're goin' to let ya get away with that?" They charged after the moles, yelling bad words, their enormous teeth flashing.

"Now is the time to use our spray, James. It has to work or we're doomed."

Neither of them had ever sprayed an enemy. Moles didn't like to use their defensive spray because it gave off a horrible danger scent. Once out of curiousity, James had tried his spray and sent the entire village running for emergency tunnels. The gophers were dangerously close.

"Wait until they're upon us. Now!" Stewart shouted, "Give it to them."

The gophers coughed and struggled for breath and were blinded for a few moments as the stinky spray engulfed them. In the confusion, the two moles slipped past the gang and raced far into the tunnel until they no longer could hear the gophers' curses and screams.

CHAPTER SIX
THE SPRING

They stopped to rest, panting with fear, but pleased that they had escaped the gopher gang. Stewart studied their position, scratching a map in the ground.

"We must dig down."

"How far?" James knew no moles who had ever dug farther than three feet into the earth.

"According to the Ordinance Map, we'll have to go two more feet down to get to the spring bed," Stewart said with a sigh.

They found some larvae and divided it, eating quickly. Then the digging began. They shovelled out the dirt into shafts that made huge mounds above ground. They went deeper, deeper into the earth.

"It's gloomy here, much darker." James could hear his voice echo back. "And it smells awfully musty. Are there any bad things down here? Hope we find this spring soon."

Just as he spoke they heard running water. It was the spring! They were next to the line of rocks and mud which kept the spring on course. The brothers had to burrow through this wall to set the spring free. They dug and dug, their bodies aching, through the cracks between the rocks, weakening the wall until the faint sound of water became louder, then roared. The wall crumbled in a heap! The spring was released, but they were swept along with it!

"Help, Stewart," screamed James, his fat little body whirling around and around in the water.

"Try to keep your head up. I'm coming." The gush of water forced the two moles back toward the gopher tunnel. Stewart stopped himself by grabbing onto a tree root and caught James by his back paw. They struggled to hold on as the water rushed by, taking all in its path.

Just when they thought they could hang on no longer, a flat board flushed from above ground, floated by.

"Jump! Now!" Stewart yelled above the roar of the water.

Miraculously, they landed on their backs on the board, which took off at amazing speed through the gophers' tunnel.

They swirled past the gopher gang stranded on a ledge. The gang shouted and threw sticks at them. Gripping the board tightly, the two moles sped on through the tunnel, which grew wider and wider. Suddenly, a huge wave rolled over them.

All was quiet. They had been washed up at the edge of the field which was slowly filling with water.

"What happened?" coughed James, water pouring out of his mouth.

"We did it! We did it!" Stewart yelled, clapping his paws in excitement. "Now all we have to do is get across the field before it floods."

Their excitement turned to horror as they saw the sky changing from black to gray. It was growing light. The sun would blind them completely and would bring out the humans, their enemies.

"We still have time. Hurry before the light gets us." Stewart took James by the paw and they stumbled along, feeling their way. The red rim of the sun was over the horizon. They heard the humans as they crept past the machines.

"What's this, a flood? We can't work here." A rush of spit from the human's mouth landed on the brothers' tails making them jump. "Houses can never be built on this land. Got to get these machines out before we're stuck." The humans were too busy to notice the furry little animals scurrying past.

As the sun rose, it struck the moles with pain. They saw streaks and sparks but little else. Soon they would not be able to move at all. Putting their paws on the ground for vibrations, they heard a mole voice squeak, "There they are." It was Police Chief Black, Papa and a search party. The brothers were carried home.

CHAPTER SEVEN
HEROES

The brothers slept for two mole days. They woke to the delicious smell of earthworm pancakes. Papa and Mama were standing beside their beds. Both of them waited for Papa to scold them for going above ground. Instead they were hugged and kissed, again and again. They even were excused from school.

Then Mama changed the bandage on Stewart's tummy. He was surprised that it didn't hurt at all.

"You were very brave and very clever," Papa said. "We know what you did. Police Chief Black heard the humans talking. You saved us all. The town wants to have a celebration to honour you."

Mama clapped her paws with joy. "You were magnificent!" she said proudly.

James thought that must mean great. When things settled down, he would look up 'magnificent' in The Noah Webster Unabridged Dictionary for Moles.

The celebration was more exciting than they had ever dreamed. The village's main tunnel was blocked off from the usual digging. Led by the Mole School Band, Stewart and James rode on the backs of the Mole Police through the tunnel, while the entire village cheered and threw bits of rootlets.

The parade ended in front of the town hall. A giant larva cake had been placed on a banquet table. After everyone had eaten, Mayor Burrows called the brothers up to the speaker's platform. As the band played and everyone cheered, the brothers smiled at each other, glad that Mama had brushed their fur and bought them new jackets.

Mayor Burrows presented the two little moles with golden medals. On the front of the medals was a picture of a stream and on the back was the date of their heroic act.

"But for you, our town would have vanished," the Mayor said as he placed the medals around the brothers' necks. "We have begun digging our beautiful shafts under the dry land beyond the flooded field, safe from all human building. Thanks to your magnificent mission, we can stay together. Mole Town will go on forever."

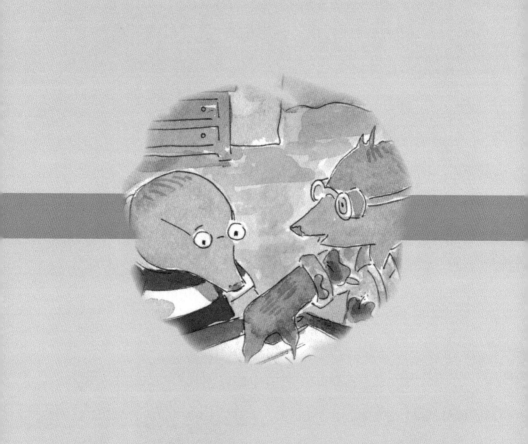

HOLEY MOLEY! A QUIZ

Burrow into your brain and dig out the answers to this quiz.

1. Who pulled the books off the library shelves at story hour?
2. What time is James Mole supposed to be in bed?
3. What does Mama Mole prepare for the brothers' dinner?
4. Where did Stewart Mole hide the Mole Ordinance Map?
5. What did the search party find of Cousin Eddie's?
6. Where did the brothers hide from the large black dog?
7. What caused Stewart Mole's injury?
8. Where does the gopher gang hang out?
9. How did the brothers escape from the gopher gang?
10. What special treat was served at the Mole Town celebration?

Check your answers on the next page.

ANSWERS TO MOLE QUIZ

1. Sam Mole
2. 7:30 p.m.
3. Earthworm casserole
4. In the breadbox
5. His broken eye glasses
6. Bulldozer scoop
7. Sharp piece of glass
8. Video arcade at edge of Mole Town
9. Used their mole spray
10. Larva cake

DRAW A PICTURE OF YOUR FAVOURITE MOLE CHARACTER OR SCENE FROM THE BOOK.

5001478R00043

Printed in Great Britain
by Amazon.co.uk, Ltd.,
Marston Gate.